Stella

Anaïs Nin

A Phoenix Paperback

Stella first published in *Winter of Artifice* by Peter Owen in 1974

This edition published in 1996 by Phoenix
a division of Orion Books Ltd
Orion House, 5 Upper St Martin's Lane, London WC2H 9EA

ISBN 1 85799 756 5

Typeset by Deltatype Ltd, Ellesmere Port, Cheshire
Printed in Great Britain by Clays Ltd, St Ives plc

Stella

Stella sat in a small, dark room and watched her own figure acting on the screen. Stella watched her 'double' moving in the light, and she did not recognize her. She almost hated her. Her first reaction was one of revolt, of rejection. This image was not she. She repudiated it. It was a work of artifice, of lighting, of stage setting.

The shock she felt could not be explained by the obvious difference between her daily self to which she purposely brought no enhancement and the screen image which was illuminated. It was not only that the eyes were enlarged and deepened, that the long eyelashes played like some Oriental latticework around them and intensified the interior light. The shock came from some violent contrast between Stella's image of herself and the projected self she could not recognize at all. To begin with, she had always seen herself in her own interior mirror, as a child woman, too small. And then this little bag of poison she carried within, the poison of melancholy and dissatisfaction she always felt must be apparent in her coloring, must produce a grey tone, or brown (the colors she wore in preference to others, the sackcloth robes of punishment). And the paralyzing fears, fear of love, fear of people coming too near (nearness brings wounds), invading her – her tensions and stage frights in the face of love . . . The first kiss for example, that first kiss which was to transport her, dissolve her, which was to swing her upward into the only paradise on earth . . . that first kiss of which she had been so frightened that at the moment of the miracle, out of panic, nerves, from her delicately shaped stomach came dark rumbling like some long-sleeping volcano becoming active.

Whereas the image on the screen was completely washed of the coloring and tones of sadness. It was imponderably light, and moved always with such a flowering of gestures that it was like the bloom and flowering of nature. This figure moved with ease, with illimitableness towards others, in a dissolution of feeling. The eyes opened and all the marvels of love, all its tonalities and nuances and multiplicities poured out as for a feast. The body danced a dance of receptivity and response. The hair undulated and swung as if it had breathing pores of its own, its own currents of life and electricity, and the hands preceded the gesture of the body like some slender orchestra leader's baton unleashing a symphony.

This was not the grey-faced child who had run away from home to become an actress, who had known hunger and limitations and obstacles, who had not yet given herself as she was giving herself on the screen. . . .

And the second shock was the response of the people.

They loved her.

Sitting next to her, they did not see her, intent on loving the woman on the screen.

Because she was giving to many what most gave to the loved one. A voice altered by love, desire, the lips forming a smile of open tenderness. They were permitted to witness the exposure of being in a moment of high feeling, of tenderness, indulgence, dreaming, abandon, sleepiness, mischievousness, which was only uncovered in moments of love and intimacy.

They received these treasures of a caressing glance, a unique tonality and voice, an intimate gesture by which we are enchanted and drawn to the one we love. This openness they were sharing was the miraculous openness and revelation which took place only in love, and it caused a current of love to flow between the audience and the woman on the screen, a current of gratitude. . . . Then this response moved like a searchlight and found her, smaller, less luminous, less open, poorer, and like some diminished image of the other, but it flowed around her, identified her. The audience came near her, touched her, asked for her signature. And she hung her head, drooped, could not accept the worship. The woman on the screen was a stranger to her. She did not see any analogy, she saw only the violent contrast which only reinforced her conviction that the screen image was illusory, artificial, artful. She was a deceiver, a pretender. The woman on the screen went continually forward, carried by her story, led by the plot loaned to her. But Stella, Stella herself was blocked over and over again by inner obstacles.

What Stella had seen on the screen, the figure of which she had been so instantaneously jealous, was the free Stella. What did not appear on the screen was the shadow of Stella, her demons, doubt and fear. And Stella was jealous. She was not only jealous of a more beautiful woman, but of a free woman. She marvelled at her own movements, their flow and ease. She marvelled at the passionate giving that came like a flood from her eyes, melting everyone, an act of osmosis. And it was to this woman men wrote letters and this woman they fell in love with, courted.

They courted the face on the screen, the face of translucence, the face of wax on which men found it possible to imprint the image of their fantasy.

No metallic eyes or eyes of crystal as in other women, but liquid, throwing a mist dew and vapor. No definite smile but a hovering, evanescent, uncapturable smile which set off all pursuits. An air of the unformed, waiting to be formed, an air of eluding, waiting to be crystallized, an air of evasion, waiting to be catalyzed. Indefinite contours, a wavering voice capable of all tonalities, tapering to a whisper, an air of flight to be captured, an air of turning corners perpetually and vanishing, some quality of matter that calls for an imprint, a carving, this essence of the feminine on which men could impose any desire, which awaited fecundation, which invited, lured, appealed, drew, ensorcelled by its seeming incompleteness, its hazy mysteries, its rounded edges.

The screen Stella with her transparent wax face, changing and changeable, promising to meet any desire, to mould itself, to respond, to invent if necessary . . . so that the dream of man like some sharp instrument knew the moment had come to imprint his most secret image . . . The image of Stella mobile, receiving the wish, the desire, the image imposed upon it.

She bought a very large, very spacious Movie Star bed of white satin.

It was not the bed of her childhood, which was particularly small because her father had said she was a pixie and she would never grow taller.

It was not the student bed on which she had slept during the years of poverty before she became a well-known actress.

It was the bed she had dreamed and placed in a setting of grandeur, it was the bed that her screen self had often been placed in, very wide and very sumptuous and not like her at all. And together with the bed she had dreamed a room of mirrors, and very large perfume bottles and a closet full of hats and rows of shoes, and the white rug and setting of a famous screen actress, altogether as it had been dreamed by so many women. And finally she had them all, and she lived among them without feeling that they belonged to her, that she had the stature and the assurance they demanded. The large bed . . . she slept in it as if she were sleeping in a screen story. Uneasily. And not until she found a way of slipping her small body away from the splendor, satin, space, did she sleep well: by covering her head.

And when she covered her head she was back in the small bed of her childhood, back in the small space of the little girl who was afraid.

The hats, properly perched on stands as in all women's dreams of an actress wardrobe, were never taken down. They required such audacity. They demanded that a role be played to its maximum perfection. So each time she had reached into the joyous hat exhibit, looked at the treasured hats, she took again the little skull cap, the unobtrusive page and choir-boy cap.

The moment when her small hand hesitated, lavishing even a caress over the arrogant feather, the challenged upward tilts, the regal velvets, the labyrinthian veils, the assertive gallant ribbons, the plumage and decorations of triumph, was it doubt which reached for the tiny skull cap of the priest, choir-boy and scholar?

Was it doubt which threw a suspicious glance over the shoes she had collected for their courage, shoes intended to walk the most entrancing and dangerous paths? Shoes of assurance and daring exploration, shoes for new situations, new steps, new places. All shined and polished for variety and change and adventure, and then each day rebuked, left like museum pieces on their shelves while she took the familiar and slightly worn ones that would not impose on her feet too large a role, too great an undertaking, shoes for the familiar route to the studio, to the people she knew well, to the places which held no surprises. . . .

Once when Stella was on the stage acting a love scene, which was taking place after a scene in a snowstorm, one of the flakes of artificial snow remained on the wing of her small and delicate nose. And then, during the exalted scene, the woman of warm snow whose voice and body seemed to melt into one's hands, the dream of osmosis, the dream of every lover, to find a substance that will confound with yours, dissolve, and yield and incorporate and become indissoluble – all during this scene there lay the snowflake catching the light and flashing signals of gently humorous inappropriateness and misplacement. The snowflake gave the scene an imperfection which touched the heart and brought all the feelings of the watchers to converge and rest upon that infinitely moving absurdity of the misplaced snowflake.

If Stella had known it she would have been crushed. The lightest of her defects, weighing no more than a snowflake, which touched the human heart as only fallibility can touch it, aroused Stella's self-condemnation and weighed down upon her soul with the oppressive weight of all perfectionism.

At times the woman on the screen and the woman she was every day encountered and fused together. And those were the moments when the impetus took its flight in full opulence and reached plenitude. They were so rare that she considered them peaks inaccessible to daily living, impossible to attain continuously.

But what killed them was not the altitude, the rarefied intensity of them. What killed them for her was that they remained unanswerable. It was a moment human beings did not feel together or in rhythm. It was a moment to be felt alone. It was the solitude that was unbearable.

Whenever she moved forward she fell into an abysm.

She remembered a day spent in full freedom by the sea with Bruno. He had fallen asleep late and she had slipped away for a swim. All through the swimming she had the impression of swimming into an ocean of feeling – because of Bruno she would no longer move separately from this great moving body of feeling undulating with her which made of her emotions an illimitable symphonic joy. She had the marvellous sensation of being a part of a vaster world and moving with it because of moving in rhythm with another being.

The joy of this was so intense that when she saw him approaching she ran towards him wildly, joyously. Coming near him like a ballet dancer she took a leap towards him, and he, frightened by her vehemence, and fearing that she would crash against him, instinctively became absolutely rigid, and she felt herself embracing a statue. Without hurt to her body, but with immeasurable hurt to her feelings.

Bruno had never seen her on the screen. He had seen her for the first time at a pompous reception where she moved among the other women like a dancer among pedestrians and distinguished herself by her mobility, by her voice which trembled and wavered, by her little nose which wrinkled when she smiled, her lips which shivered, the foreign accent which gave a hesitancy to her phrases as if she were about to make a portentous revelation, and by her hands which vibrated in the air.

He saw her in reality, yet he did not see Stella but the dream of Stella. He loved instantly a woman without fear, without doubt, and his nature, which had never taken flight, could now do so with her. He saw her in flight. He did not sense that a nature such as hers could be paralyzed, frozen with fear, could retreat, could regress, negate, and then in extreme fear, could also turn about and destroy.

For Stella this love had been born under the zodiacal sign of doubt. For Bruno, under the sign of faith.

In a setting of opulence, a setting of such elegance that it had required the wearing of one of the museum hats, the one with the regal feather, from two opposite worlds they came: Stella consumed with a hunger for love, and Bruno by the emptiness of his life.

As Stella appeared among the women, what struck Bruno was that he was seeing for the first time an animated woman. He felt caught in her current, carried. Her rhythm was contagious. He felt instantaneous obedience to her movement.

At the same time he felt wounded. Her eyes had pierced some region of his being no eyes had ever touched before. The vulnerable Bruno was captured, his moods and feelings henceforth determined, woven into hers. From the first moment they looked at each other it was determined that all she said would hurt him but that she could instantly heal him by moving one inch nearer to him. Then the hurt was instantly healed by the odor of her hair or the light touch of her hand on him.

An acute sense of distance was immediately established, such as Bruno had never known before to exist between men and women. A slight contradiction (and she loved contradiction) separated him from her and he suffered. And this suffering could only be abated by her presence and would be renewed as soon as they separated.

Bruno was discovering that he was not complete or autonomous.

Nor did Stella promise him completeness, nearness. She had the changing quality of dream. She obeyed her own oscillations. What came into being between them was not a marriage but an interplay where nothing was ever fixed. No planetary tensions, chartered and mapped and measured.

Her movements were of absolute abandon, yieldingness, and then at the smallest sign of lethargy or neglect, complete withdrawal and he had to begin courtship anew. Every day she could be won again and lost again. And the reason for her flights and departures, her breaks from him, were obscure and mysterious to him.

One night when they had been separated for many days, she received a telegram that he would visit her for a whole night. For her this whole night was as long, as portentous, as deep as a whole existence. She dwelt on every detail of it, she improvised upon it, she constructed and imagined and lived in it completely for many days. This was to be their marriage.

Her eyes overflowed with expectancy as she met him. Then she noticed that he had come without a valise. She did not seek the cause. She was struck by this as a betrayal of their love. Her being closed with an anguish inexplicable to him (an anguish over the possibility of a break, a separation, made her consider every small break, every small separation like a premonition of an ultimate one).

He spent his time in a struggle to reassure her, to reconquer her, to renew her faith, and she in resisting. She considered the demands of reality as something to be entirely crushed in favor of love, that obedience to reality meant a weakness in love.

Reality was the dragon that must be killed by the lover each time anew. And she was blind to her own crime against love, corroding it with the acid of her own doubt.

But a greater obstacle she had yet to encounter.

At the first meeting the dream of their encounter eclipsed the surrounding regions of their lives and isolated them together as inside a cocoon of silk and sensation. It gave them the illusion that each was the center of the other's existence.

No matter how exigent was the demand made upon Stella by her screen work, she always overthrew every obstacle in favor of love. She broke contracts easily, sailed at a moment's notice, and no pursuit of fame could interfere with the course of love. This willingness to sacrifice external achievements or success to love was typically feminine but she expected Bruno to behave in the same manner.

But he was a person who could only swim in the ocean of love if his moorings were maintained, the long established moorings of marriage and children. The stately house of permanency and continuity that was his home, built around his role in the world, built on peace and faith, with the smile of his wife which had become for him the smile of his mother – this edifice made out of the other components of his nature, his need for a haven, for children who were as his brothers had been, for a wife who was that which his mother had been. He could not throw over all these creations and possessions of his day for a night's dream, and Stella was that night's dream, all impermanency, vanishing and returning only with the night.

She, the homeless one, could not respect that which he respected. He, by respecting the established, felt free of guilt. He was paying his debt of honor and he was free, free to adore her, free to dream her. This did not appease her Nor the simplicity with which he explained that he could not tear from its foundation the human home, with the children and the wife whom he protected. He could only love and live in peace if he fulfilled his promises to what he had created.

It was not that Stella wanted the wife's role or place. She knew deep down how unfitted she was for this role and to that side of his nature. It was merely that she could not share a love without the feeling that into this region of Bruno's being she did not care to enter, that there lay there a danger of death to their relationship. For her, any opening, any unconquered region contained the hidden enemy, the seed of death, the possible destroyer. Only absolute possession calmed her fear.

He was at peace with his conscience and therefore he feared no punishment for the joys she gave him. It was a condition of his nature. Because he had not destroyed or displaced, he felt he would not be destroyed or displaced and he could give his faith and joy to the dream. Her anguish and fears were inexplicable to him. For him there was no enemy ready to spring at her from the calm of his house.

If a telephone call or some emergency at home tore him away from her, for her it was abandon, and the end of love. If the time were shortened it signified a diminishing of love. If a choice were to be made she felt that he would choose his wife and children against her. None of these fatalistic signs were visible to him.

This hotel room was for him the symbol of the freedom of their love, the voyage, the exploration, the unknown, the restlessness that could be shared together; the surprises, the marvellously formless and bodiless and houseless freedom of this world created by two people in a hotel room. It was outside of the known, the familiar, and built only out of intensity, the present, with the great exalted beauty of the changing, the fluctuating, the dangerous and unmoored. . . .

Would she destroy this world created only on the fragrance of a voice, enhanced by intermittent disappearances? The privilege of travelling further into space and wonder because free of ballast? This marvellous world patterned only according to the irregularities of a dream, with its dark abysms in between, its change and flow and capriciousness?

Bruno clung desperately to the beauty, to the preciousness of this essence, pure because it was an essence. And for

 him even less threatened by death than his first love had

been by the development of daily life. (For at a certain moment the face of his wife was no longer the face of a dream but became the face of his mother. At the same moment as the dream died, his home became the human and dreamless home of his boyhood, his children became the playmates of his adolescence.)

And Stella, when he explained this, knew the truth of it, yet she was the victim of a stronger demon, a demon of doubt blindly seeking visible proofs, the proofs of the love in reality which would most effectively destroy the dream. For passion usually has the instinctive wisdom to evade the test of human life together which is only possible to love. For Stella, because of her doubt, so desperately in need of reassurance, if he surrendered all to her it would mean that he was giving all his total love to their dream, whereas to him surrendering all meant giving Stella a lesser self (since passion was the love of the dreamed self and not the reality).

There was in this hotel room stronger proof of the strength of the dream, and Stella demanded proofs of its human reality and in so doing exposed its incompleteness, and hastened its end (Pandora's box).

Stella! he always cried out as he entered, enveloping her in the fervor of his voice.

Stella! he repeated, to express how she filled his being and overflowed within him, to fill the room with this name which filled him.

He had a way of saying it which was like crowning her

the favorite. He made of each encounter such a rounded, complete experience, charged with the violence of a great hunger. Not having seen her upon awakening, not having helped to free her of the cocoon web of the night, not having shared her first contact with daylight, her first meal, the inception of her moods for that day, the first intentions and plans for action, he felt all the more impelled to catch her at the moment of the climax, to join her at the culmination. The lost, missed moments of life together, the lost, missed gestures, were thrown in desperation to feed the bonfire known only to foreshortened lives.

Because of all this that was lost around the love, the hotel room became the island, the poem and the paradise, because of all that was torn away, and sunk away.

The miracle of intensification.

Yet Stella asked, mutely, with every gasp of doubt and anguish: Let us live together (as if human life would give a certitude!). And he answered, mutely, with every act of faith: Let us dream together!

He arrived each day with new eyes. Undimmed by familiarity. New eyes for the woman he had not seen enough. New, intense, deeply seeing eyes, seeing her in her entirety each time like a new person.

As he did not see the process of her walking towards their island, dressing for it, resting for it, fighting off the inundation and demands of other people to reach him, her presence seemed like an apparition, and he had to repossess her, because apparitions tend to disappear as they come, by routes unknown, into countries unknown.

There was between them this knowledge of the missing dimension and the need to recapture the lost terrain, to play the emotional detective for the lost fragments of the selves which had lived alone, as separate pieces, in a great effort to bring them all together into one again.

At his wrists the hair showed brilliant gold.

Hers dark and straight, and his curled, so that at times it seemed it was his hair which enveloped her, it was his desire which had the feminine sinuosities to espouse and cling, while hers was rigid.

It was he who surrounded and enveloped her, as his curled hair wound around the straightness of hers, and how sweet this had been in her distress and her chaos. She touched his wrists always in wonder, as if to ascertain his presence, because the joyousness of his coloring delighted her, because the smoothness of his movements was a preliminary to their accord and rhythms. Their movements toward each other were symphonic and preordained. Her divination of his moods and his of hers synchronized their movements like those of a dance. There were days when she felt small and weak, and he then increased his stature to receive and shelter her, and his arms and body seemed a fortress, and there were days when he was in need of her strength, days when their mouths transmitted all the fevers and hungers, days when frenzy called for an abandon of the whole body. Days when the caresses were a drug, or a symphony, or small secret duets and duels, or vast complex veilings which neither could entirely tear apart, and there were secrets, and resistances, and frenzies, and again dissolutions from which it seemed as if neither could ever return to the possession of his independence.

There was always this mingling of hairs, which later in the bath she would tenderly separate from hers, laying the tendrils before her like the signs of the calendar of their love, the unwitherable flowers of their caresses.

While he was there, melted by his eyes, his voice, sheltered in his tallness, encompassed by his attentiveness, she was joyous. But when he was gone, and so entirely gone that she was forbidden to write him or telephone him, that she had in reality no way to reach him, touch him, call him back, then she became possessed again with this frenzy against barriers, against limitations, against forbidden regions. To have touched the point of fire in him was not enough. To be his secret dream, his secret passion. She must ravage and conquer the absolute, for the sake of love. Not knowing that she was at this moment the enemy of love, its executioner.

Once he stood about to depart and she asked him: can't you stay for the whole night? And he shook his head sadly, his blue eyes no longer joyous, but blurred. This firmness with which she thought he was defending the rights of his wife, and with which in reality he only defended the equilibrium of his scrupulous soul, appeared to her like a flaw in the love.

If Stella felt an obstacle placed before one of her wishes such as her wish that Bruno should stay the whole night with her when it was utterly impossible for him to do so, this obstacle, no matter of what nature, became the symbol of a battle she must win or else consider herself destroyed.

She did not pause to ask herself the reasons for the refusal, or to consider the validity of these reasons, the claims to which others may have had a right. The refusal represented for her the failure to obtain a proof of love. The removal of this obstacle became a matter of life and death, because for her it balanced success or failure, abandon or treachery, triumph or power.

The small refusal, based on an altogether separate reason, unrelated to Stella, became the very symbol of her inner sense of frustration, and the effort to overcome it the very symbol of her salvation.

If she could bend the will and decision of Bruno, it meant that Bruno loved her. If not, it meant Bruno did not love her. The test was as devoid of real meaning as the tearing of leaves on a flower done by superstitious lovers who place their destiny in the mathematics of coincidence or accident.

And Stella, regardless of the cause, became suddenly blind to the feelings of everyone else as only sick people can become blind. She became completely isolated in this purely personal drama of a refusal she could not accept and could not see in any other light but that of a personal offense to her. A love that could not overcome all obstacles (as in the myths and legends of romantic ages) was not a love at all.

(This small favor she demanded took on the proportions of the ancient holocausts demanded by the mystics as proofs of devotion.)

She had reached the exaggeration, known to the emotionally unstable, of considering every small act as an absolute proof of love or hatred, and demanding of the faithful an absolute surrender. In every small act of yielding Stella accumulated defenses against the inundating flood of doubts. The doubt devoured her faster than she could gather external proofs of reassurance, and so the love given her was not a free love but a love that must accumulate votive offerings like those made by the primitives to their jealous gods. There must be every day the renewal of candles, foods and precious gifts, incense and sacrifice and if necessary (and it was always necessary to the neurotic) the sacrifice of human life. Every human being who fell under her spell became not the lover, but the day and night nurse to this sickness, this unfillable longing, this ravenous devourer of human happiness.

You won't stay all night?

The muted, inarticulate despair these few words contained. The unheard, unnoticed, unregistered cry of loneliness which arises from human beings. And not a loneliness which could be appeased with one night, or with a thousand nights, or with a lifetime, or with a marriage. A loneliness that human beings could not fill. For it came from her separation from human beings. She felt her separation from human beings and believed the lover alone could destroy it.

The doubt and fear which accompanied this question made her stand apart like some unbending god of ancient rituals watching for this accumulation of proofs, the faithful offering food, blood and their very lives. And still the doubt was there for these were but external proofs and they proved nothing. They could not give her back her faith.

The word penetrated Stella's being as if someone had uttered for the first time the name of her enemy, until then unknown to her.

Doubt. She turned this word in the palm of her dreaming hands, like some tiny hieroglyph with meaning on four sides.

From some little tunnel of obscure sensations there came almost imperceptible signs of agitation.

She packed hurriedly, crushing the hat with the feather, breaking his presents.

Driving fast in her very large, too large, her movie star car, driving fast, too fast away from pain, the water obscured her vision of the road and she set the wipers in motion. But it was not rain that clouded the windows.

*

In her movie star apartment there was a small turning stairway like that of a lighthouse leading to her bedroom, which was watched by a tall window of square glass bricks. These shone like a quartz cave at night. It was the prism which threw her vision back into seclusion again, into the wall of the self.

It was the window of the solitary cell of the neurotic.

One night when Bruno had written her that he would telephone her that night (he had been banished once again, and once again had tried to reconquer her) because he sensed that his voice might accomplish what his note failed to do, at the moment when she knew he would telephone, she installed a long concerto on the phonograph and climbed the little stairway and sat on the step.

No sooner did the concerto begin to spin than the telephone rang imperatively.

Stella allowed the music to produce its counter-witchcraft. Against the mechanical demand of the telephone, the music spiralled upward like a mystical skyscraper, and triumphed. The telephone was silenced.

But this was only the first bout. She climbed another step of the stairway and sat under the quartz window, wondering if the music would help her ascension away from the warmth of Bruno's voice.

In the music there was a parallel to the conflict which disturbed her. Within the concerto too the feminine and the masculine elements were interacting. The trombone, with its assertions, and the flute, with its sinuosities. In this transparent battle the trombone, in Stella's ears and perhaps because of her mood, had a tone of defiance which was almost grotesque. In her present mood the masculine instrument would appear as a caricature!

And as for the flute, it was so easily victimized and overpowered. But it triumphed ultimately because it left an echo. Long after the trombone had had its say, the flute continued its mischievous, insistent tremolos.

The telephone rang again. Stella moved a step farther up the stairs. She needed the stairs, the window, the concerto, to help her reach an inaccessible region where the phone might ring as any mechanical instrument, without reverberating in her being. If the ringing of the telephone had caused the smallest tremor through her nerves (as the voice of Bruno did) she was lost. Fortunate for her that the trombone was a caricature of masculinity, that it was an inflated trombone, drowning the sound of the telephone. So she smiled one of her eerie smiles, pixen and vixen too, at the masculine pretensions. Fortunate for her that the flute persisted in its delicate undulations, and that not once in the concerto did they marry but played in constant opposition to each other throughout.

The telephone rang again, with a dead, mechanical persistence and no charm, while the music seemed to be pleading for a subtlety and emotional strength which Bruno was incapable of rivalling. The music alone was capable of climbing those stairways of detachment, of breaking like the waves of disturbed ocean at her feet, breaking there and foaming but without the power to suck her back into the life with Bruno and into the undertows of suffering.

She lay in the darkness of her white satin bedroom, the mirrors throwing aureoles of false moonlight, the rows of perfume bottles creating false suspended gardens.

The mattress, the blankets, the sheets had a lightness like her own. They were made of the invisible material which had once been pawned off on a gullible king. They were made of air, or else she had selected them out of familiar, weighty materials and then touched them with her aerial hands. (So many moments when her reality was questionable – the time she leaped out of her immense automobile, and there on the vast leather seat lay such a diminutive pocketbook as no woman could actually use, the pocketbook of a midget. Or the time she turned the wheel with two fingers. There is a lightness which belongs to other races, the race of ballet dancers.)

Whoever touched Stella was left with the tactile memory of down and bonelessness, as after touching the most delicate of Persian cats.

Now lying in the dark, neither the softness of the room nor its whiteness could exorcise the pain she felt.

Some word was trying to come to the surface of her being. Some word had sought all day to pierce through like an arrow the formless, inchoate mass of incidents of her life. The geological layers of her experience, the accumulated faces, scenes, words and dreams. One word was being churned to the surface of all this torment. It was as if she were going to name her greatest enemy. But she was struggling with the fear we have of naming that enemy. For what crystallized simultaneously with the name of the enemy was an emotion of helplessness against him! What good was naming it if one could not destroy it and free one's self? This feeling, stronger than the desire to see the face of the enemy, almost drowned the insistent word into oblivion again.

What Stella whispered in the dark with her foreign accent enhancing strongly, markedly the cruelty of the sound was:

ma soch ism

Soch! Och! It was the och which stood out, not ma or ism but the och! which was like some primitive exclamation of pain. Am, am I, am I, am I, am I, whispered Stella, am I a masochist?

She knew nothing about the word except its current meaning: 'voluntary seeking of pain.' She could go no further into her exploration of the confused pattern of her life and detect the origin of the suffering. She could not, alone, catch the inception of the pattern, and therefore gain power over this enemy. The night could not bring her one step nearer to freedom. . . .

A few hours later she watched on the screen the story of Atlantis accompanied by the music of Stravinski.

First came a scene like a Paul Klee, wavering and humid, delicate and full of vibrations. The blue, the green, the violet were fused in tonalities which resembled her feeling, all fused together and so difficult to unravel. She responded with her answering blood rhythms, and with the same sense she always had of herself possessing a very small sea, something which received and moved responsively in rhythm. As if every tiny cell were not separated by membranes, as if she were not made of separate nerves, sinews, blood vessels, but one total fluid component which could flow into others, divine their feelings, and flow back again into itself, a component which could be easily moved and penetrated by others like water, like the sea.

When she saw the Paul Klee scene on the screen she instantly dissolved. There was no more Stella, but a fluid component participating at the birth of the world. The paradise of water and softness.

But upon this scene came the most unexpected and terrifying explosion, the explosion of the earth being formed, broken, reformed and broken anew into its familiar shape.

This explosion Stella was familiar with and had expected. It reverberated in her with unexpected violence. As if she had already lived it.

 Where had she experienced before this total annihilation

of a blue, green and violet paradise, a paradise of welded cells in a perpetual flow and motion, that this should seem like the second one, and bring about such a painful, physical memory of disruption?

As the explosions came, once, twice, thrice, the peace was shattered and blackened, the colors vanished, the earth muddied the water, the annihilation seemed total.

The earth reformed itself. The water cleared. The colors returned. A continent was born above.

In Stella the echo touched a very old, forgotten region. Through layers and layers of time she gazed at an image made small by the distance: a small figure. It is her childhood, with its small scenery, small climate, small atmosphere. Stella was born during the war. But for the diminutive figure of the child the war between parents – all division and separation – was as great as the world war. The being, small and helpless, was torn asunder by the giant figures of mythical parents striving and dividing. Then it was nations striving and dividing. The sorrow was transferred, enlarged. But it was the same sorrow: it was the discovery of hatred, violence, hostility. It was the dark face of the world, which no childhood was ever prepared to receive. In the diminutive and fragile vessel of childhood lies the paradise that must be destroyed by explosions, so that the earth may be created anew. But the first impact of hatred and destruction upon the child is sometimes too great a burden on its innocence. The being is sundered as the earth is by earthquakes, as the soul cracks under violence and hatred. Paradise (the sense of Paul Klee) was from the first intended to be swallowed by the darkness.

As Stella felt the explosions, through the microscope of her emotions carried backwards, she saw the fragments of the dispersed and sundered being. Every little piece now with a separate life. Occasionally, like mercury, they fused, but they remained elusive and unstable. Corroding in the separateness.

Faith and love united her to human beings as a child. She was known to have walked the streets at the age of six inviting all the passersby to a party at her home. She hailed carriages and asked the driver to drive 'to where there were many people.'

The first explosion. The beginning of the world. The beginning of a pattern, the beginning of a form, a destiny, a character. Something which always eludes the scientists, the tabulators, the detectives. We catch a glimpse of it, like this, through the turmoil of the blood which remembers the seismographic shocks.

Stella could not remember what she saw in the mirror as a child. Perhaps a child never looks at the mirror. Perhaps a child, like a cat, is so much inside of itself it does not see itself in the mirror. She sees a child. The child does not remember what he looks like.

Later she remembered what she looked like. But when she looked at photographs of herself at one, two, three, four, five years, she did not recognize herself. The child is one. At one with himself. Never outside of himself.

She could remember what she did, but not the reflection of what she did. No reflections. Six years old. Seven years old. Eight years old. Eleven. No image. No reflection. But feeling.

In the mirror there never appeared a child. The first mirror had a frame of white wood. In it there was no Stella. A girl of fourteen portraying Joan of Arc, La Dame Aux Camélias, Peri Banu, Carlota, Electra.

No Stella, but a diguised actress multiplied into many personages. Was it in these games that she had lost her vision of her true self? Could she only win it again by acting? Was that why now she refused every role – every role that did not contain at least one aspect of herself? But because they contained only one aspect of herself they only emphasized the dismemberment. She would get hold of one aspect, and not of the rest. The rest remained unlived.

The first mirror in which the self appears is very large, inlaid in a brown wood wall. Next to it a window pours down so strong a light that the rest of the room is in complete darkness, and the image of the girl who approaches the mirror is brought into luminous relief. It is the first spotlight, actually, the first aureole of lighting, bringing her into relief, but in a state of humiliation. She is looking at her dress, a dress of shiny, worn, dark blue serge which has been fixed up for her out of an old one belonging to a cousin. It does not fit her. It is meager, it looks poor and shrunk. The girl looks at the blue dress with shame.

It is the day she has been told at school that she is gifted for acting. They had come purposely into the class to tell her. She who was always quiet and did not wish to be noticed, was told to come and speak to the Drama teacher before everyone, and to bear the compliment on her first performance. And the joy, the dazzling joy which first struck her was instantly killed by the awareness of the dress. She did not want to get up, to be noticed. She was ashamed of the meager dress, its worn, its orphan air.

She can only step out of this image, this dress, this humiliation by becoming someone else. She becomes Melisande, Sarah Bernhardt, Faust's Marguerite, La Dame Aux Camélias, Thais. She is decomposed before the mirror into a hundred personages, and recomposed into paleness, immobility and silence.

She will never wear again the shrunken worn serge cast-off dress, but she will often wear again this mood, this feeling of being misrepresented, misunderstood, of a false appearance, of an ugly disguise. She was called and made visible to all, out of her shyness and withdrawal, and what was made visible was a girl dressed like an orphan and not in the costume of wonder which befitted her.

She rejects all the plays. Because they cannot contain her. She wants to walk into her own self, truly presented, truly
 revealed. She wants to act only herself. She is no longer an

actress willing to disguise herself. She is a woman who has lost herself and feels she can recover it by acting this self. But who knows her? What playwright knows her? Not the men who loved her. She cannot tell them. She is lost herself. All that she says about herself is false. She is misleading and misled. No one will admit blindness.

No one who does not have a white cane, or a seeing eye dog will admit blindness. Yet there is no blindness or deafness as strong as that which takes place within the emotional self.

Seeing has to do with awareness, the clarity of the senses is linked to the spiritual vision, to understanding. One can look back upon a certain scene of life and see only a part of the truth. The characters of those we live with appear with entire aspects missing, like the missing arms or legs of unearthed statues. Later, a deeper insight, a deeper experience will add the missing aspects to the past scene, to the lost character only partially seen and felt. Still later another will appear. So that with time, and with time and awareness only, the scene and the person become complete, fully heard and fully seen.

Inside of the being there is a defective mirror, a mirror distorted by the fog of solitude, of shyness, by the climate inside of this particular being. It is a personal mirror, lodged in every subjective, interiorized form of life.

Stella received a letter from Laura, her father's second wife.

'Come immediately. I am divorcing your father.'

Her father was an actor. In Warsaw he had achieved fame and adulation. He had remained youthful and the lover of all women. Stella's mother, whose love for him had encompassed more than the man, permitted him great freedom. It was not his extravagant use of this freedom which had killed her feeling for him, but his inability to make her feel at the center of his life, feel that no matter what his peripheries she remained at the center. In exchange for her self-forgetfulness he had not been able to give anything, only to take. He had exploited the goodness, the largeness, the voluntary blindness. He had dipped into the immense reservoir of her love without returning to it an equal flow of tenderness, and so it had dried. The boundlessness of her love was to him merely an encouragement of his irresponsibility. He thought it could be used infinitely, not knowing that even an infinite love needed nourishment and fecundation; that no love was ever self-sustaining, self-propelling, self-renewing.

And then one day her love died. For twenty years she had nourished it out of her own substance, and then it died. His selfishness withered it. And he was surprised. Immensely surprised, as if she had betrayed him.

She had left with Stella. And another woman had come, younger, a disciple of his, who had taken up the burden of being the lover alone. Stella knew the generosity of the

 second wife, the devotion. She knew how deeply her father

must have used the reservoir to empty it. How deeply set his pattern of taking without giving. Again the woman's love was emptied, burnt out.

'He threatens to commit suicide,' wrote Laura, 'but I do not believe it.' Stella did not believe it either. He loved himself too well.

Stella's father met her at the station. In his physical appearance there was clearly manifested the fact that he was not a man related to others but an island. In his impeccable dress there was a touch of finite contours. His clothes were of an insulating material. Whatever they were made of, they gave the impression of being different materials from other people's, that the well pressed lines were not intended to be disturbed by human hands. It was sterilized elegance conveying his uniqueness, and his perfectionism. If his clothes had not carried this water-repellent, feeling-repellent quality of perfection, his eyes would have accomplished this with their expression of the island. Distinctly, the person who moved toward him was an invader, the ship which entered this harbor was an enemy, the human being who approached him was violating the desire of islands to remain islands. His eyes were isolated. They created no warm bridges between them and other eyes. They flashed no signal of welcome, no light of response, and above all they remained as closed as a glass door.

He wanted Stella to plead with Laura. 'Laura suspects me

of having an affair with a singer. She has never minded before. And this time it happens not to be true. I dislike being . . . exiled unjustly. I cannot bear false accusations. Why does she mind now? I can't understand. Please go and tell her I will spend the rest of my life making her happy. Tell her I am heartbroken.' (As he said these words he took out his silver cigarette case and noticing a small clouded spot on it he carefully polished it with his handkerchief.) 'I've been unconscious. I didn't know she minded. Tell Laura I had nothing to do with this woman. She is too fat.'

'But if you had,' said Stella, 'wouldn't it be better to be truthful this time? She is angry. She will hate a lie now more than anything. Why aren't you sincere with her? She may have proofs.'

At the word proof his neat, alert head perked, cool, collected, cautious, and he said: 'What proofs? She can't have proofs. I was careful. . . .'

He is still lying, thought Stella. He is incurable.

She visited Laura, who was small and childlike. She was like a child who had taken on a maternal role in a game, and found it beyond her strength. Yet she had played this role for ten years. Almost like a saint, the way she had closed her eyes to all his adventures, the way she had sought to preserve their life together. Her eyes always believing, diminishing the importance of his escapades, disregarding gossip, blaming the women more often than him.

 Today as she received Stella, for whom she had always

had a strong affection, these same believing eyes were changed. There is nothing clearer than the mark of a wound in believing eyes. It shows clear and sharp, the eyes are lacerated, they seem about to dissolve with pain. The soft faith was gone. And Stella knew instantly that her pleading was doomed.

'My father's unfaithfulness meant nothing. He always loved you above all others. He was light, but his deep love was for you. He was irresponsible, and you were too good to him, you never rebelled.'

But Laura defended her attitude: 'I am that kind of person. I have great faith, great indulgence, great love. For that reason if someone takes advantage of this I feel betrayed and I cannot forgive. I have warned him gently. I was not ill over his infidelities but over his indelicacies. I wanted to die. I hoped he would be less obvious, less insolent. But now it is irrevocable. When I added up all his selfish remarks, his reckless gestures, the expression of annoyance on his face when I was ill, his indifferences to my sadness, I cannot believe he ever loved me. He told me such impossible stories that he must have had a very poor idea of my judgment. Until now my love was strong enough to blind me . . . but now, understand me, Stella, I see everything. I remember words of his he uttered the very first day. The kind of unfaithfulness women can forgive is not the kind your father was guilty of. He was not unfaithful by his interest in other women, but he betrayed what we had together: he abandoned me spiritually and emotionally. He did not feel for me. Another thing I cannot forgive him. He was not a natural man, but he was posing as an ideal being. He covered acts which were completely selfish under a coat of altruism. He even embroidered so much on this role of ideal being that I had all the time the deep instinct that I was being cheated, that I was living with a man who was acting. This I can't forgive. Even today he continues to lie. I have definite proofs. They fell into my hands. I didn't want them. And then he was not content with having his mistress live near me, he still wanted me to invite her to my house, he even taunted me for not liking her, not fraternizing with her. Let him cry now. I have cried for ten years. I know he won't kill himself. He is acting. He loves himself too much. Let him now measure the strength of this love he destroyed. I feel nothing. Nothing. He has killed my love so completely I do not even suffer. I never saw a man who could kill a love so completely. I say a man! I often think he was a child, he was as irresponsible as a child. He was a child and I became a mother and that is why I forgave him everything. Only a mother forgives everything. The child, of course, doesn't know when he is hurting the mother. He does not know when she is tired, sick; he does nothing for her. He takes it for granted that she is willing to die for him. The child is passive, yielding, and accepts everything, giving nothing in return but affection. If the mother weeps he will throw his arms around her and then he will go out and do exactly what caused her to weep. The child never thinks of the mother except as the all-giver, the all-forgiving, the indefatigable love. So I let my husband be the child. . . . But he, Stella, he was not even tender like a child, he did not give me even the kind of love a child has for the mother. There was no tenderness in him!' And she wept. (He had not wept.)

As Stella watched her she knew the suffering had been too great and that Laura's love was absolutely broken.

When she returned to her father carrying the word 'irrevocable' to him, her father exclaimed: 'What happened to Laura? Such a meek, resigned, patient, angelical woman. A little girl, full of innocence and indulgence. And then this madness. . . .'

He did not ask himself, he had never asked himself, what he must have done to destroy such resignation, such innocence, such indulgence. He said: 'Let's look at our house for the last time.'

Until now it had been their house. But in reality the house belonged to Laura and she asked her husband not to enter it again, to make a list of his belongings and she would have them sent to him.

They stood together before the house and looked up at the window of his room: 'I will never see my room again. It's incredible. My books are still in there, my photographs, my clothes, my scrap books, and I . . .'

At the very moment they stood there a slight earthquake had been registered in Warsaw. At that very moment when her father's life was shaken by the earthquake of a woman's rebellion, when he was losing love, protection, faithfulness, luxury, faith. His whole life disrupted in a moment of feminine rebellion. Earth and the woman, and this sudden rebellion. On the insensitive instrument of his egoism no sign had been registered of this coming disruption.

As he stood there looking at his house for the last time the bowels of the earth shook. Laura was quietly weeping while his life cracked open and all the lovingly collected possessions fell into an abysm. The earth opened under his perpetually dancing feet, his waltzes of courtship, his contrapuntal love scenes.

In one instant it swallowed the colorful ballet of his lies, his pointed foot evasions, his vaporous escapes, the stage lights and halos with which he surrounded and disguised his conquests and appetites. Everything was destroyed in the tumult. The earth's anger at his lightness, his audacities, his leaps over reality, his escapes. His house cracked open and through the fissures fell his rare books, his collection of paintings, his press notices, the gifts from his admirers.

But before this happened the earth had given him so many warnings. How many times had he not seen the glances of pain in Laura's eyes, how many times had he overlooked her loneliness, how many times had he pretended not to hear the quiet weeping from her room, how many times had he failed in ordinary tenderness . . . before the revolt.

'And if if I get sick,' he said, walking away from his house, 'who will take care of me? If only I could keep the maid Lucille. She was wonderful. There never was anyone like her. She was the only one who knew how to press my summer suits. With her all my problems would be solved. She was silent and never disturbed me and she never left the house. Now I don't know if I will be able to afford her. Because if I have her it will mean I will have to have two maids. Yes, two, because Lucille is not a good enough cook.'

Sadly he walked down the street with Stella's arm under his. And then he added; 'Now that I won't have the car any more, I will miss the Fête des Narcisses at Montreux, and I am sure I would have got the prize this year.'

While he balanced himself on the tightrope of his delusions, Stella had no fear for him. He could see no connection between his behavior and Laura's rebellion. He could not see how the most trivial remarks and incidents could accumulate and form a web to trap him. He did not remember the trivial remark he made to the maid who was devotedly embroidering a nightgown for Laura during one of her illnesses. He had stood on the threshold watching and then said with one of his characteristic pirouettes: 'I know someone on whom this nightgown would look more beautiful. . . .' This had angered the loyalty of the maid and later influenced her to crystallize the proofs against him. Everyone around him had taken the side of the human being he overlooked because they could see so obviously the enormous disproportion between her behavior towards him and his towards her. The greater her love, almost, the greater had grown his irresponsibility and devaluation of this love.

What Stella feared was a moment of lucidity, when he might see that it was not the superficial aspect of his life which had destroyed its basic foundation, but his disregard of and undermining of the foundation.

For the moment he kept himself balanced on his tightrope.

In fact he was intently busy placing himself back on a pedestal. He was now the victim of an unreasonable woman. Think of a woman who bears up with a man for ten years, and then when he is about to grow old, about to grow wise and sedentary, about to resign from his lover's career, then she revolts and leaves him alone. What absolute illogicality!

'For now,' he said, 'I am becoming a little tired of my love affairs. I do not have the same enthusiasms.'

After a moment of walking in silence he added: 'But I have you, Stella.'

The three loves of his life. And Stella could not say what she felt: 'You killed my love too.'

Yet at this very moment she remembered when it happened. She was then a little girl of twelve. Her father and mother were separated and lived in opposite sections of the city. Once a week Stella's mother allowed her to visit her father. Once a week she was plunged from an atmosphere of poverty and struggle to one of luxury and indolence. Such a violent contrast that it came with a shock of pain.

Once when she was calling on her father she saw Laura there for the first time. She heard Laura laugh. She saw her tiny figure submerged in furs and smelled her perfume. She could not see her as a woman. She seemed to her another little girl. A little girl dressed and hairdressed like a woman, but laughing, and believing and natural. She felt warmly towards her, did not remember that she was the one replacing her mother, that her mother would expect her to hate the intruder. Even to this child of twelve it was clear that it was Laura who needed the protection, that she was not the conqueror. That in the suave, charming, enchanting manners of her actor father there lurked many dangers for human beings, for the vulnerable ones especially. The same danger as had struck her mother and herself: danger of abandon and loneliness.

Laura too was looking at Stella with affection. Then she whispered to her father and Stella with her abnormally sensitive hearing caught the last words, 'buy her stockings.'

(From then on it was Laura who assumed all her father's sentimental obligations, it was Laura who sent gifts to his mother, to her later.)

The father and daughter went off together through the most beautiful shopping streets of Warsaw. She had become acutely aware of her mended stockings now that Laura had noticed them. Her father would be ashamed of walking with her. But he did not seem concerned. He was walking now with the famous grace that the stage had so much enhanced, a grace which made it appear that when he bowed, or kissed a hand, or spoke a compliment, he was doing it with his whole soul. It gave to his courtships such a romantic totality that a mere bow over a woman's hand took on the air of a ceremony in which he laid his life at her feet.

He entered a luxurious cane shop. He had the finest canes spread before him. He selected the most precious of all woods, and the most delicately carved. He asked Stella for her approval. He emptied his pocketbook, saying: 'I can still take you home in a cab.' And he took her home in a cab. With his new, burnished cane he pointed out Stella's drab house to the cabman. With a gesture of romantic devotion, as if he were laying a red carpet under her feet, he delivered her to her poverty, to the aggressions of creditors, to the anxieties, the humiliations, the corroding pain of everyday want.

Today she was not walking with her father in mended stockings. But she was riding in taxis like an ambassador between Laura and her father. Laura sent her father an intricate Venetian vase on an incredibly slender stem which could not be entrusted to the moving van. Stella was

 holding it in one hand, her muff in the other, and at her feet lay packages of old love letters. And her father sent her back in the same taxi with a locket, a ring, photographs, letters.

Stella attended the thousandth performance of a play called *The Orphan* in which her father starred.

'*The Orphan*,' he said, 'that suits me well now, that is how I feel, abandoned by Laura.' And speaking of the orphan, he the orphan, the abandoned one, the victim for the first time, he wept. (But not over Laura's pain, or broken faith.)

In the middle of the performance, when he was sitting in an armchair and speaking, suddenly his arms fell, and he sat stiffly back. It was so swift, so brusque, that he looked like a broken marionette. No man could break this way, so sharply, so absolutely. People rushed on the stage. 'It's a heart attack,' said the doctor.

Stella accompanied him to his house. He lay rigid as in death.

She could not weep. For him, yes, for his sadness. Not for her father. All links were broken. But a man, yes, any man who suffered. The darling of women. White hair and elegance. Solitude. All the women around him and none near enough. Stella unable to move nearer, because none could move nearer to him. He barred the way with his self-love. His self-love isolated him. Self-love the watchman, barring all entrance, all communication. One could not console him. He was dying because with the end of luxury, protection, of his role, his life ends. He took all his sustenance from woman but he never knew it.

It was not Stella who killed him. She had not been the one to say: you killed my love.

Pity convulsed her, but she could do nothing. He was fulfilling his destiny. He had sought only his pleasure. He was dying alone on the stage of self-pity.

But when he was lying down on a bench in the dressing room, his collar for the first time carelessly open, the fat doctor listening to his heart (breaking with self-pity), so slender, so stylized, so meticulously chiselled, like an effigy, a burning pity choked her.

Someone whose every word she had hated, whose every act and thought she condemned, whose every mannerism was false, every gesture a role, yet because this figure lay on a couch dying of self-pity, lay with his eyes closed in a supreme comedian's act, Stella could love and pity again. Does the love of the father never die, even when it is buried a million times under stronger loves, even when she had looked at him without illusion? The figure, the slenderness of the body, the fineness of its form, still escaped from the dark tomb of buried love and was alive, because he had so artfully lain down like a victim, fainted before a thousand people, because he had been an actor until the end; as for Laura, and Stella's mother – no one had seen or heard them weep.

A fragile Stella, lying in her ivory satin bed, amongst mirrors.

Her eloquent body can speak out all the feelings in the language of the dance. Now her hands lie tired on her knees, tired and defeated.

Her dance is perpetually broken by the wounds of love.

In her white nightgown she does not look like an enchantress but like an orphan.

In her white nightgown she runs out of her room downstairs to spare the servants an added fatigue, she the exhausted one.

Her body and face so animated that they do not seem made of flesh, but like antennae, breath, nerve.

Delicate, she lies back like a tired child, but so knowing.

Bright, she speaks as she feels, always.

Unreal – her voice vanishes to a whisper, as if she herself were going to vanish and one must hold one's breath to hear her.

Oriental, she takes the pose of the Bali dancers. Her head always free from her body like the bird's head so free from its fragile stem.

The language of her hands. As they curve, leap, circle, trepidate, one fears they will always end clasped in a prayer that no one should hurt her.

No role could contain her intensity.

She gave off such a brilliance in acting it was unbearable. Too great an exaltation for the role, which breaks like too small a vessel. Too great a warmth. The role was dwarfed, was twisted and lost. When she begged for the roles which could contain this intensity they were denied her.

Off the stage she contained the same mischievous wrinkling of her little nose, the same entranced eyes, the child's ease and grace and impulsiveness (in the most pompous restaurant of the city she reached out towards a passing silver tray carried by a pompous waiter and stole a fried potato).

The intensity made the incidents she portrayed seem inadequate and small. There was a glow from so deep a source of feeling that it drowned the mediocre personages of the Hollywood gallery.

She ate like a child, avidly, as if in fear that it would be taken away from her, forbidden her by some parent. Like the child, she had no coquetry. She was unconscious of her tangled hair and liked her face washed of make-up. If someone made love to her while she still carried the weight of wax on her eyelashes, if someone made love to her artificially exaggerated eyelashes, she was offended, as if by a betrayal.

She was a child carrying a very old soul and burdened with it, and wishing to deposit it in some great and passionate role. In Joan of Arc, or Marie Bashkirtseff . . . or Rejane, or Eleonora Duse.

There are those who disguise themselves, like Stella's father, who disguised himself and acted what he was not. But Stella only wanted to transform and enlarge herself and wanted to act only what she felt she was, or could be. And Hollywood would not let her. Hollywood had its sizes and standards of characters. One could not transgress certain limited standard sizes.

Philip. When Stella first saw him she laughed at him. He was too handsome. She laughed: 'Such a wonderful Don Juan plumage,' she said, and turned away. The Don Juan plumage had never charmed her.

But the next morning she saw him walking before her, holding himself as in a state of euphoria. She was still mocking his magnificence. But as he passed her, with a free, large, lyrical walk, he smiled at his companion so brilliant a smile, so wild, so sensual that she felt a pang. It was the smile of joy, a joy unknown to her.

At the same time she took a deeper breath into her lungs, as if the air had changed, become free of suffocating fogs, noxious poisons.

He was at first impenetrable to her, because the climate of lightness was anew to her.

She glided on the wings of his smile and his humor.

When she left him she heard the wind through the leaves like the very breath of life and again she breathed the large free altitudes where anguish cannot reach to suffocate.

She followed with him the capricious outlines of pure desire, trusting his smile.

The pursuit of joy. She possessed his smile, his eyes, his

assurance. There are beings who come to one to the tune of music. She always expected him to appear in a sleigh, to the tune of sleigh bells. As a child she had heard sleigh bells and thought: they have the sound of joy. When she opened his cigarette case she expected the tinkling, light, joyous music of music boxes.

The absence of pain must mean it was not love but an enchantment. He came bringing joy and when he left she felt it was to go to his mysterious source and fetch some more. She waited without impatience and without fear. He was replenishing his supply. And every object he came in contact with was charged with the music that causes gaiety to flower.

The knowledge that he was coming held her in a suspense of pleasure, that of a high, perilous trapeze leap. The long intervals between their meetings, the absence of love, made it like some brilliant trapeze incident, spangled, accompanied by music. She could admire their deftness and accuracy in keeping themselves outside of the circle of pain. The little seed of anguish to which she was so susceptible could not germinate in this atmosphere.

She laughed when he confessed to her his Don Juan fatigues, the exigencies of the role women imposed upon him. 'Women keep such strict accounts and compare notes to see if you are always at the same level!' A weary Don Juan resting his head upon her knees. As if he knew that for her, awake or asleep, he was always the magician of joy.

He bore no resemblance to any other person or moment of her life. She felt as if she had escaped from a fatal, repetitious pattern.

One evening Stella entered a restaurant alone and was seated at the side of Bruno. So much time had passed and she felt herself in another world, yet the sight of Bruno caused her pain. He was deeply disturbed.

They sat together and lingered over the dinner.

At midnight Stella was to meet Philip. At eleven-thirty when she began to gather her coat, Bruno said: 'Let me see you home.'

Thinking of the possibility of an encounter between him and Philip (at midnight Philip was coming to her place), she showed hesitation. This hesitation caused Bruno such acute pain that he began to tremble. At all cost, she felt, he must not know . . . So she said quickly: 'I'm not going home. I'm expected at some friends'. I forgot them when I saw you. But I promised to drop in.'

'Can I take you there?'

She thought: if I mention friends he knows, he will come with me. She said: 'Just put me in a taxi.'

This reawakened his doubts. Again a look of pain crossed his face, and Stella was hurt by it, so she said hastily and spontaneously: 'You can take me there. It's on East Eighty-ninth.'

While he talked tenderly in the taxi, she thought

desperately that she must find a house with two entrances, of which there are many on Fifth Avenue, but as she had never been on East Eighty-ninth Street, she wondered what she would find on the corner, perhaps a club, or a private house, or a Vanderbilt mansion.

From the taxi window she looked anxiously at the big, empty lot on the right and the private house on the left. Bruno's voice so vulnerable, her fear of hurting him. Time pressing, and Philip waiting for her before the door of her apartment. Then she signalled the driver to stop before an apartment house on the corner of Eighty-ninth Street and Madison Avenue.

Then she kissed Bruno lightly but was startled when he stepped out with her and dismissed the taxi. 'I need a walk,' he said.

First of all the front door was locked and she had to ring for the doorman whom she had not expected to see quite so soon. As she continued to walk into the hallway, he asked. 'Who do you want to see? Where are you going?'

She could only say: 'There is a door on Madison Avenue?' This aroused his suspicion and he answered roughly: 'Why do you want to know? Who do you want to see?'

'Nobody,' said Stella. 'I just came in here because there was a man following me and annoying me. I thought I might walk through and slip out of the other entrance and get a cab and go home.'

'That door is locked for the night. You can't go through there.'

'Very well, then, I'll wait here for a while until that man leaves.'

The doorman could see through the door the figure of Bruno walking back and forth. What had happened? Was he considering trying to find her? Did he believe she had no friends in this house and that he would catch her coming out again? Was he intuitively jealous and wondering if his intuition was right? Waiting. He waited there, smoking, walking in the snowy night. She was sitting in the red-carpeted hall, in a red plush chair, while the doorman paced up and down, and Bruno paced up and down before the house.

Thinking of Philip waiting for her, sitting there, heart beating and pounding, mind whirling.

She stood up and walked cautiously to the door and saw Bruno still walking in the cold.

Pain and laughter, pain out of the old love for Bruno, laughter from some inner, secret sense of playing with difficulties.

She said to the doorman: 'That man is still there. Listen, I must get away somehow. You must do something for me.'

Not too gallantly, he called the elevator boy. The elevator boy took her down the cellar, through a labyrinth of grey hallways. Another elevator boy joined them. She told them about the man who followed her, adding details to the story.

Passing trunks, valises, piles of newspapers, and rows and rows of garbage cans, then bowing their heads, they passed through one more alleyway, up some stairs and unlocked the back door.

One of the boys went for a taxi. She thanked them, with the gaiety of a child in a game. They said it was a great pleasure and that New York was a hell of a place for a lady.

In the taxi she lay low on the seat so that Bruno could not see her as they passed Madison Avenue.

Philip was in a state of anxiety over her lateness.

She wanted to say: you are not the one who should be anxious! It is you I came back to! I struggled to get to you. But I'm here. And Bruno it is who is standing outside, waiting in the cold.

One day Philip asked her to wait for him in his apartment because his train had been delayed. (Before that he had always come to her). For the first time he wanted to find her there, in his own home.

She had never entered his bedroom.

It was the first time she stepped out of the ambience he created for her by his words, stories, actions. The missing dimensions of Philip she knew must exist but he had known how to keep them invisible.

And now late at night, out of idleness, out of restlessness, fumbling very much like the blind person left for the first time to himself, she began to caress the objects he lived with, at first with a tenderness, because they were his, because she still expected them to emit a melody for her, to open up with playful surprises, to yield to her finger an immediate proof of love. But none of them emitted any sound resembling him . . . And slowly her fingers grew less caressing, grew awkward. Her fingers recognized objects made for or given by women. Her fingers recognized the hairpins of the wife, the powder box of the wife, and books with dedications by women, the photographs of women. The fingerprints on every object were women's fingerprints.

Then in the bedroom she stared at his dressing table. She stared at an immaculate and 'familiar' set of silver toilet articles. It was not that Philip had a wife, and mistresses, and belonged to the public which awakened her. It was the silver toilet set on the dressing table, a replica of the artistocratic one which had charmed her childhood. Equally polished, equally symmetrically arranged. She was certain that if she lifted the hair brush it would be fragrant. Of course, it was fragrant.

The silver toilet set of her father had reappeared. And then of course, it made the analogy more possible. Everything else was there too – the wife, and the public, and the mistresses.

Her father receiving applause and the flowers of all women's tribute, the flowers of their femininity with the fern garnishings of multicolored hair given prodigally to the stage figures – the illusion needed for desire already artificially prepared for those too lazy to prepare their own. (In the love we have for those who are not on the stage the illusion has to be created by the love. The people who fall in love with the performers are like those who fall in love with magicians; they are the ones who cannot create the illusion or magic with the love – the mise-en-scene, the producer, the music, the role, which surrounds the personage with all that desire requires.)

In this love Philip will receive bouquets from women, and Stella will find again the familiar pain her father had given her, which she didn't want.

Because they had touched the ring around the planet of love, the outer ring of desire, had taken graceful leaps across visitless weeks, she had believed these to be marvelous demonstrations of their agility to escape the prisons of deep love's pains.

There were days when she felt: the core of this drama of mine is that at an early age I lost the element of joy. (In childhood we glimpse paradise, its possibility, we exist in it.) At what moment was it lost and replaced by anguish? Could she remember?

Standing before the silver brushes, combs and boxes on Philip's dressing table she remembered that just as other people watch the sun and rain for barometers to their moods, she had run every day to watch these silver objects.

 When her father was in stormy periods and ready to leave

the house, they were disarranged and clouded. When he was in full bloom of success, harmony and pleasure they were symmetrically placed, and highly polished. The initials shone with exquisite iridescence. And on days of great discord and tragedy they disappeared altogether and were placed in their niches in his valise. So she consulted them like the barometers of her emotional climate.

When he left the house altogether it seemed as if none of the objects that remained possessed this power to gleam, to shed a brilliance. It was a transition from phosphorescence to continuous greyness.

It was when he left that her life changed color. Because he took only the pleasure, he also shed this pleasure around him. When she was thrust out of this effulgence and away from the gleam of beautiful objects, she was thrust into sadness.

How could joy have vanished with the father?

A person could walk away without carrying everything away with him. He might have left a little casket from which she could draw joy at will! He could have left the silver toilet set. But no, he took everything away with him because he took away the faith, her faith in love, and left her the prey of doubts and fears.

Human beings have a million little doorways of communication. When they feel threatened they close them, barricade themselves. Stella closed them all. Suffocation set in. Asphyxiation of the feelings.

She appeared in a new story on the screen. Her face was immobile like a mask. It was not Stella. It was the other shell of Stella.

People sent her enormous bouquets of rare flowers. Continued to send them. She signed the receipts, she even signed notes of thanks. Flowers for the dead, she murmured. With only a little wire, and a round frame, they would do as well.

A Note on Anaïs Nin

Anaïs Nin, 1903–77, American diarist, novelist and critic, was born in Neuilly, just outside Paris. Her father was a Spanish composer, her mother half-French and half-Danish. In 1914 she moved with her mother to New York, where she lived until returning to Paris in 1923. In her early life she was a model, dancer, teacher and lecturer, and she later became a practising psychoanalyst under the tutelage of Otto Rank. She began writing her renowned *Diary* (10 vols., 1966–83) in 1931; her first publication was an essay entitled *D. H. Lawrence: An Unprofessional Study* (Paris, 1932). She turned to fiction with the novel *House of Incest* (Paris, 1936; USA, 1947). Prominent in Paris literary circles, she became the friend of Henry Miller and Lawrence Durrell. At the beginning of World War II she returned to the USA. Her subsequent work includes a collection of three novelettes, *The Winter of Artifice* (Paris, 1939; USA, 1942), a volume of short stories, *Under a Glass Bell* (1944), and the novels *Ladders to Fire* (1946), *Children of the Albatross* (1947), *The Four-Chambered Heart* (1950), *A Spy in the House of Love* (1954), *Solar*

Baroque (1958) and *Collages* (1964). Her volumes of erotica include *Delta of Venus: Erotica* (1977) and *Little Birds* (1979). Her critical studies are *Realism and Reality* (1946), *On Writing* (1947) and *The Novel of the Future* (1968).

Other titles in this series

JANE AUSTEN *Catharine*
MAEVE BINCHY *Cross Lines*
CLARE BOYLAN *The Stolen Child*
EDNA O'BRIEN *Mrs Reinhardt*
KATE CHOPIN *Athénaïse*
COLETTE *The Kepi*
ANITA DESAI *Scholar and Gypsy*
MARIA EDGEWORTH *The Lottery*
GEORGE ELIOT *Brother Jacob*
JANET FRAME *The Reservoir*
ELIZABETH GASKELL *Half a Life-Time Ago*
ELIZABETH JANE HOWARD *Mr Wrong*
A.L. KENNEDY *Tea and Biscuits*
DORIS LESSING *The Pit*
KATHERINE MANSFIELD *At the Bay*
DAPHNE DU MAURIER *The Birds*
ANAÏS NIN *Stella*
ROSAMUNDE PILCHER *The Key*
KATE PULLINGER *Forcibly Bewitched*

Ruth Rendell *Ginger and the Kingsmarkham Chalk Circle*
Michèle Roberts *God's House*
Rose Tremain *The Kite Flyer*
Penny Vincenzi *The Glimpses*
Fay Weldon *Heat Haze*
Edith Wharton *The Letters*